Henry James OM (15 April 1843 – 28 February 1916) was an American-British author regarded as a key transitional figure between literary realism and literary modernism, and is considered by many to be among the greatest novelists in the English language. He was the son of Henry James Sr. and the brother of renowned philosopher and psychologist William James and diarist Alice James.

He is best known for a number of novels dealing with the social and marital interplay between émigré Americans, English people, and continental Europeans. Examples of such novels include The Portrait of a Lady, The Ambassadors, and The Wings of the Dove. His later works were increasingly experimental. In describing the internal states of mind and social dynamics of his characters, James often made use of a style in which ambiguous or contradictory motives and impressions were overlaid or juxtaposed in the discussion of a character's psyche.(Source: Wikipedia)

Literary works:
Watch and Ward (1871)
Roderick Hudson (1875)
The American (1877)
The Europeans (1878)
Confidence (1879)
Washington Square (1880)
The Portrait of a Lady (1881)
The Bostonians (1886)
The Princess Casamassima (1886)
The Reverberator (1888)
The Tragic Muse (1890)
The Other House (1896)
The Spoils of Poynton (1897)
What Maisie Knew (1897)

THE
MARRIAGES

HENRY JAMES

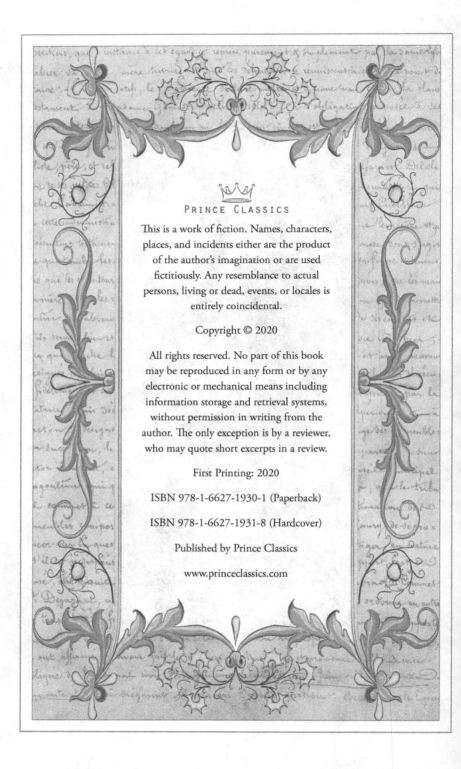

Contents

THE
MARRIAGES

I

"WON'T you stay a little longer?" the hostess asked while she held the girl's hand and smiled. "It's too early for every one to go—it's too absurd." Mrs. Churchley inclined her head to one side and looked gracious; she flourished about her face, in a vaguely protecting sheltering way, an enormous fan of red feathers. Everything in her composition, for Adela Chart, was enormous. She had big eyes, big teeth, big shoulders, big hands, big rings and bracelets, big jewels of every sort and many of them. The train of her crimson dress was longer than any other; her house was huge; her drawing-room, especially now that the company had left it, looked vast, and it offered to the girl's eyes a collection of the largest sofas and chairs, pictures, mirrors, clocks, that she had ever beheld. Was Mrs. Churchley's fortune also large, to account for so many immensities? Of this Adela could know nothing, but it struck her, while she smiled sweetly back at their entertainer, that she had better try to find out. Mrs. Churchley had at least a high-hung carriage drawn by the tallest horses, and in the Row she was to be seen perched on a mighty hunter. She was high and extensive herself, though not exactly fat; her bones were big, her limbs were long, and her loud hurrying voice resembled the bell of a steamboat. While she spoke to his daughter she had the air of hiding from Colonel Chart, a little shyly, behind the wide ostrich fan. But Colonel Chart was not a man to be either ignored or eluded.

"Of course every one's going on to something else," he said. "I believe there are a lot of things to-night."

"And where are *you* going?" Mrs. Churchley asked, dropping her fan and turning her bright hard eyes on the Colonel.

"Oh I don't do that sort of thing!"—he used a tone of familiar resentment that fell with a certain effect on his daughter's ear. She saw in it that he thought Mrs. Churchley might have done him a little more justice. But what made the honest soul suppose her a person to look to for a perception of fine shades? Indeed the shade was one it might have been a little difficult to seize—the difference between "going on" and coming to a dinner of twenty people. The pair were in mourning; the second year had maintained it for Adela, but the Colonel hadn't objected to dining with Mrs. Churchley, any more than he had objected at Easter to going down to the Millwards', where he had met her and where the girl had her reasons for believing him to have known he should meet her. Adela wasn't clear about the occasion of their original meeting, to which a certain mystery attached. In Mrs. Churchley's exclamation now there was the fullest concurrence in Colonel Chart's idea; she didn't say "Ah yes, dear friend, I understand!" but this was the note of sympathy she plainly wished to sound. It immediately made Adela say to her "Surely you must be going on somewhere yourself."

"Yes, you must have a lot of places," the Colonel concurred, while his view of her shining raiment had an invidious directness. Adela could read the tacit implication: "You're not in sorrow, in desolation."

Mrs. Churchley turned away from her at this and just waited before answering. The red fan was up again, and this time it sheltered her from Adela. "I'll give everything up—for *you*," were the words that issued from behind it. "*Do* stay a little. I always think this is such a nice hour. One can really talk," Mrs. Churchley went on. The Colonel laughed; he said it wasn't fair. But their hostess pressed his daughter. "Do sit down; it's the only time to have any talk." The girl saw her father sit down, but she wandered away, turning her back and pretending to look at a picture. She was so far from agreeing with Mrs. Churchley that it was an hour she particularly disliked. She was conscious of the queerness, the shyness, in London, of the gregarious flight of guests after a dinner, the general *sauve qui peut* and panic fear of being left with the host and hostess. But personally she always felt the contagion, always conformed to the rush. Besides, she knew herself turn red now, flushed with a conviction that had come over her and that she wished not to show.

Her father sat down on one of the big sofas with Mrs. Churchley; fortunately he was also a person with a presence that could hold its own. Adela didn't care to sit and watch them while they made love, as she crudely imaged it, and she cared still less to join in their strange commerce. She wandered further away, went into another of the bright "handsome," rather nude rooms—they were like women dressed for a ball—where the displaced chairs, at awkward angles to each other, seemed to retain the attitudes of bored talkers. Her heart beat as she had seldom known it, but she continued to make a pretence of looking at the pictures on the walls and the ornaments on the tables, while she hoped that, as she preferred it, it would be also the course her father would like best. She hoped "awfully," as she would have said, that he wouldn't think her rude. She was a person of courage, and he was a kind, an intensely good-natured man; nevertheless she went in some fear of him. At home it had always been a religion with them to be nice to the people he liked. How, in the old days, her mother, her incomparable mother, so clever, so unerring, so perfect, how in the precious days her mother had practised that art! Oh her mother, her irrecoverable mother! One of the pictures she was looking at swam before her eyes. Mrs. Churchley, in the natural course, would have begun immediately to climb staircases. Adela could see the high bony shoulders and the long crimson tail and the universal coruscating nod wriggle their horribly practical way through the rest of the night. Therefore she *must* have had her reasons for detaining them. There were mothers who thought every one wanted to marry their eldest son, and the girl sought to be clear as to whether she herself belonged to the class of daughters who thought every one wanted to marry their father. Her companions left her alone; and though she didn't want to be near them it angered her that Mrs. Churchley didn't call her. That proved she was conscious of the situation. She would have called her, only Colonel Chart had perhaps dreadfully murmured "Don't, love, don't." This proved he also was conscious. The time was really not long—ten minutes at the most elapsed—when he cried out gaily, pleasantly, as if with a small jocular reproach, "I say, Adela, we must release this dear lady!" He spoke of course as if it had been Adela's fault that they lingered. When they took leave she gave Mrs. Churchley, without intention and without defiance, but from the simple sincerity of her pain, a longer look into the eyes than she had ever given her before. Mrs. Churchley's onyx pupils reflected the question as distant dark windows reflect the sunset; they seemed to say: "Yes, I *am*, if that's what you want to know!"

What made the case worse, what made the girl more sure, was the silence preserved by her companion in the brougham on their way home.

They rolled along in the June darkness from Prince's Gate to Seymour Street, each looking out of a window in conscious prudence; watching but not seeing the hurry of the London night, the flash of lamps, the quick roll on the wood of hansoms and other broughams. Adela had expected her father would say something about Mrs. Churchley; but when he said nothing it affected her, very oddly, still more as if he had spoken. In Seymour Street he asked the footman if Mr. Godfrey had come in, to which the servant replied that he had come in early and gone straight to his room. Adela had gathered as much, without saying so, from a lighted window on the second floor; but she contributed no remark to the question. At the foot of the stairs her father halted as if he had something on his mind; but what it amounted to seemed only the dry "Good-night" with which he presently ascended. It was the first time since her mother's death that he had bidden her good-night without kissing her. They were a kissing family, and after that dire event the habit had taken a fresh spring. She had left behind her such a general passion of regret that in kissing each other they felt themselves a little to be kissing her. Now, as, standing in the hall, with the stiff watching footman—she could have said to him angrily "Go away!"—planted near her, she looked with unspeakable pain at her father's back while he mounted, the effect was of his having withheld from another and a still more slighted cheek the touch of his lips.

He was going to his room, and after a moment she heard his door close. Then she said to the servant "Shut up the house"—she tried to do everything her mother had done, to be a little of what she had been, conscious only of falling woefully short—and took her own way upstairs. After she had reached her room she waited, listening, shaken by the apprehension that she should hear her father come out again and go up to Godfrey. He would go up to tell him, to have it over without delay, precisely because it would be so difficult. She asked herself indeed why he should tell Godfrey when he hadn't taken the occasion—their drive home being an occasion—to tell herself. However, she wanted no announcing, no telling; there was such a horrible clearness in her mind that what she now waited for was only to be sure her father wouldn't proceed as she had imagined. At the end of the minutes she saw this particular danger was over, upon which she came out and made her own way to her brother. Exactly what she wanted to say to him first, if their parent counted on the boy's greater indulgence, and before he could say anything, was: "Don't forgive him; don't, don't!"

He was to go up for an examination, poor lad, and during these weeks his lamp burned till the small hours. It was for the Foreign Office, and there was to be some frightful number of competitors; but Adela had great hopes of him—she believed so in his talents and saw with pity how hard he worked. This would have made her spare him, not trouble his night, his scanty rest, if anything less dreadful had been at stake. It was a blessing however that one could count on his coolness, young as he was—his bright good-looking discretion, the thing that already made him half a man of the world. Moreover he was the one who would care most. If Basil was the eldest son—he had as a matter of course gone into the army and was in India, on the staff, by good luck, of a governor-general—it was exactly this that would make him comparatively indifferent. His life was elsewhere, and his father and he had been in a measure military comrades, so that he would be deterred by a certain delicacy from protesting; he wouldn't have liked any such protest in an affair of *his*. Beatrice and Muriel would care, but they were too young to speak, and this was just why her own responsibility was so great.

Godfrey was in working-gear—shirt and trousers and slippers and a beautiful silk jacket. His room felt hot, though a window was open to the summer night; the lamp on the table shed its studious light over a formidable heap of text-books and papers, the bed moreover showing how he had flung himself down to think out a problem. As soon as she got in she began. "Father's going to marry Mrs. Churchley, you know."

She saw his poor pink face turn pale. "How do you know?"

"I've seen with my eyes. We've been dining there—we've just come home. He's in love with her. She's in love with *him*. They'll arrange it."

"Oh I say!" Godfrey exclaimed, incredulous.

"He will, he will, he will!" cried the girl; and with it she burst into tears.

Godfrey, who had a cigarette in his hand, lighted it at one of the candles on the mantelpiece as if he were embarrassed. As Adela, who had dropped into his armchair, continued to sob, he said after a moment: "He oughtn't to—he oughtn't to."

"Oh think of mamma—think of mamma!" she wailed almost louder than was safe.

"Yes, he ought to think of mamma." With which Godfrey looked at the tip of his cigarette.

"To such a woman as that—after *her*!"

"Dear old mamma!" said Godfrey while he smoked.

Adela rose again, drying her eyes. "It's like an insult to her; it's as if he denied her." Now that she spoke of it she felt herself rise to a height. "He rubs out at a stroke all the years of their happiness."

"They were awfully happy," Godfrey agreed.

"Think what she was—think how no one else will ever again be like her!" the girl went on.

"I suppose he's not very happy now," her brother vaguely contributed.

"Of course he isn't, any more than you and I are; and it's dreadful of him to want to be."

"Well, don't make yourself miserable till you're sure," the young man said.

But Adela showed him confidently that she *was* sure, from the way the pair had behaved together and from her father's attitude on the drive home. If Godfrey had been there he would have seen everything; it couldn't be explained, but he would have felt. When he asked at what moment the girl had first had her suspicion she replied that it had all come at once, that evening; or that at least she had had no conscious fear till then. There had been signs for two or three weeks, but she hadn't understood them—ever since the day Mrs. Churchley had dined in Seymour Street. Adela had on that occasion thought it odd her father should have wished to invite her, given the quiet way they were living; she was a person they knew so little. He

14

had said something about her having been very civil to him, and that evening, already, she had guessed that he must have frequented their portentous guest herself more than there had been signs of. To-night it had come to her clearly that he would have called on her every day since the time of her dining with them; every afternoon about the hour he was ostensibly at his club. Mrs. Churchley *was* his club—she was for all the world just like one. At this Godfrey laughed; he wanted to know what his sister knew about clubs. She was slightly disappointed in his laugh, even wounded by it, but she knew perfectly what she meant: she meant that Mrs. Churchley was public and florid, promiscuous and mannish.

"Oh I daresay she's all right," he said as if he wanted to get on with his work. He looked at the clock on the mantel-shelf; he would have to put in another hour.

"All right to come and take darling mamma's place—to sit where *she* used to sit, to lay her horrible hands on *her* things?" Adela was appalled—all the more that she hadn't expected it—at her brother's apparent acceptance of such a prospect.

He coloured; there was something in her passionate piety that scorched him. She glared at him with tragic eyes—he might have profaned an altar. "Oh I mean that nothing will come of it."

"Not if we do our duty," said Adela. And then as he looked as if he hadn't an idea of what that could be: "You must speak to him—tell him how we feel; that we shall never forgive him, that we can't endure it."

"He'll think I'm cheeky," her brother returned, looking down at his papers with his back to her and his hands in his pockets.

"Cheeky to plead for *her* memory?"

"He'll say it's none of my business."

"Then you believe he'll do it?" cried the girl.

"Not a bit. Go to bed!"

15

"*I'll* speak to him"—she had turned as pale as a young priestess.

"Don't cry out till you're hurt; wait till he speaks to *you*."

"He won't, he won't!" she declared. "He'll do it without telling us."

Her brother had faced round to her again; he started a little at this, and again, at one of the candles, lighted his cigarette, which had gone out. She looked at him a moment; then he said something that surprised her. "Is Mrs. Churchley very rich?"

"I haven't the least idea. What on earth has that to do with it?"

Godfrey puffed his cigarette. "Does she live as if she were?"

"She has a lot of hideous showy things."

"Well, we must keep our eyes open," he concluded. "And now you *must* let me get on." He kissed his visitor as if to make up for dismissing her, or for his failure to take fire; and she held him a moment, burying her head on his shoulder.

A wave of emotion surged through her, and again she quavered out: "Ah why did she leave us? Why did she leave us?"

"Yes, why indeed?" the young man sighed, disengaging himself with a movement of oppression.

II

ADELA was so far right as that by the end of the week, though she remained certain, her father had still not made the announcement she dreaded. What convinced her was the sense of her changed relations with him—of there being between them something unexpressed, something she was aware of as she would have been of an open wound. When she spoke of this to Godfrey he said the change was of her own making—also that she was cruelly unjust to the governor. She suffered even more from her brother's unexpected perversity; she had had so different a theory about him that her disappointment was almost an humiliation and she needed all her fortitude to pitch her faith lower. She wondered what had happened to him and why he so failed her. She would have trusted him to feel right about anything, above all about such a question. Their worship of their mother's memory, their recognition of her sacred place in their past, her exquisite influence in their father's life, his fortune, his career, in the whole history of the family and welfare of the house—accomplished clever gentle good beautiful and capable as she had been, a woman whose quiet distinction was universally admired, so that on her death one of the Princesses, the most august of her friends, had written Adela such a note about her as princesses were understood very seldom to write: their hushed tenderness over all this was like a religion, and was also an attributive honour, to fall away from which was a form of treachery. This wasn't the way people usually felt in London, she knew; but strenuous ardent observant girl as she was, with secrecies of sentiment and dim originalities of attitude, she had already made up her mind that London was no treasure-house of delicacies. Remembrance there was hammered thin—to be faithful was to make society gape. The patient dead were sacrificed; they had no shrines, for people were literally ashamed of mourning. When they had hustled all sensibility out of their lives they invented the fiction that they felt too much to utter. Adela said nothing to her sisters; this reticence was part of the virtue it was her idea to practise for them. *She* was to be their mother, a direct deputy and representative. Before the vision of that other woman parading in such a character she felt capable of ingenuities, of deep diplomacies. The essence of these indeed was just tremulously to watch her father. Five days after they had dined together at Mrs. Churchley's he asked her if she had been to see that lady.

"No indeed, why should I?" Adela knew that he knew she hadn't been, since Mrs. Churchley would have told him.

"Don't you call on people after you dine with them?" said Colonel Chart.

"Yes, in the course of time. I don't rush off within the week."

Her father looked at her, and his eyes were colder than she had ever seen them, which was probably, she reflected, just the way hers appeared to himself. "Then you'll please rush off to-morrow. She's to dine with us on the 12th, and I shall expect your sisters to come down."

Adela stared. "To a dinner-party?"

"It's not to be a dinner-party. I want them to know Mrs. Churchley."

"Is there to be nobody else?"

"Godfrey of course. A family party," he said with an assurance before which she turned cold.

The girl asked her brother that evening if *that* wasn't tantamount to an announcement. He looked at her queerly and then said: "*I've* been to see her."

"What on earth did you do that for?"

"Father told me he wished it."

"Then he *has* told you?"

"Told me what?" Godfrey asked while her heart sank with the sense of his making difficulties for her.

"That they're engaged, of course. What else can all this mean?"

"He didn't tell me that, but I like her."

"*Like* her!" the girl shrieked.

"She's very kind, very good."

"To thrust herself upon us when we hate her? Is that what you call kind? Is that what you call decent?"

"Oh *I* don't hate her"—and he turned away as if she bored him.

She called the next day on Mrs. Churchley, designing to break out somehow, to plead, to appeal—"Oh spare us! have mercy on us! let him alone! go away!" But that wasn't easy when they were face to face. Mrs. Churchley had every intention of getting, as she would have said—she was perpetually using the expression—into touch; but her good intentions were as depressing as a tailor's misfits. She could never understand that they had no place for her vulgar charity, that their life was filled with a fragrance of perfection for which she had no sense fine enough. She was as undomestic as a shop-front and as out of tune as a parrot. She would either make them live in the streets or bring the streets into their life—it was the same thing. She had evidently never read a book, and she used intonations that Adela had never heard, as if she had been an Australian or an American. She understood everything in a vulgar sense; speaking of Godfrey's visit to her and praising him according to her idea, saying horrid things about him—that he was awfully good-looking, a perfect gentleman, the kind she liked. How could her father, who was after all in everything else such a dear, listen to a woman, or endure her, who thought she pleased him when she called the son of his dead wife a perfect gentleman? What would he have been, pray? Much she knew about what any of them were! When she told Adela she wanted her to like her the girl thought for an instant her opportunity had come—the chance to plead with her and beg her off. But she presented such an impenetrable surface that it would have been like giving a message to a varnished door. She wasn't a woman, said Adela; she was an address.

When she dined in Seymour Street the "children," as the girl called the others, including Godfrey, liked her. Beatrice and Muriel stared shyly and silently at the wonders of her apparel (she was brutally over-dressed) without of course guessing the danger that tainted the air. They supposed her in their innocence to be amusing, and they didn't know, any more than she did herself, how she patronised them. When she was upstairs with them after dinner Adela could see her look round the room at the things she meant to alter—their mother's things, not a bit like her own and not good enough for her. After a quarter of an hour of this our young lady felt sure she was deciding that Seymour Street wouldn't do at all, the dear old home that had done for their mother those twenty years. Was she plotting to transport them all to her horrible Prince's Gate? Of one thing at any rate Adela was certain: her father, at that moment alone in the dining-room with Godfrey, pretending to drink another glass of wine to make time, was coming to the point, was telling the news. When they reappeared they both, to her eyes, looked unnatural: the news had been told.

She had it from Godfrey before Mrs. Churchley left the house, when, after a brief interval, he followed her out of the drawing-room on her taking her sisters to bed. She was waiting for him at the door of her room. Her father was then alone with his *fiancée*—the word was grotesque to Adela; it was already as if the place were her home.

"What did you say to him?" our young woman asked when her brother had told her.

"I said nothing." Then he added, colouring—the expression of her face was such—"There was nothing to say."

"Is that how it strikes you?"—and she stared at the lamp.

"He asked me to speak to her," Godfrey went on.

"In what hideous sense?"

"To tell her I was glad."

"And did you?" Adela panted.

"I don't know. I said something. She kissed me."

"Oh how *could* you?" shuddered the girl, who covered her face with her hands.

20

"He says she's very rich," her brother returned.

"Is that why you kissed her?"

"I didn't kiss her. Good-night." And the young man, turning his back, went out.

When he had gone Adela locked herself in as with the fear she should be overtaken or invaded, and during a sleepless feverish memorable night she took counsel of her uncompromising spirit. She saw things as they were, in all the indignity of life. The levity, the mockery, the infidelity, the ugliness, lay as plain as a map before her; it was a world of gross practical jokes, a world *pour rire*; but she cried about it all the same. The morning dawned early, or rather it seemed to her there had been no night, nothing but a sickly creeping day. But by the time she heard the house stirring again she had determined what to do. When she came down to the breakfast-room her father was already in his place with newspapers and letters; and she expected the first words he would utter to be a rebuke to her for having disappeared the night before without taking leave of Mrs. Churchley. Then she saw he wished to be intensely kind, to make every allowance, to conciliate and console her. He knew she had heard from Godfrey, and he got up and kissed her. He told her as quickly as possible, to have it over, stammering a little, with an "I've a piece of news for you that will probably shock you," yet looking even exaggeratedly grave and rather pompous, to inspire the respect he didn't deserve. When he kissed her she melted, she burst into tears. He held her against him, kissing her again and again, saying tenderly "Yes, yes, I know, I know." But he didn't know else he couldn't have done it. Beatrice and Muriel came in, frightened when they saw her crying, and still more scared when she turned to them with words and an air that were terrible in their comfortable little lives: "Papa's going to be married; he's going to marry Mrs. Churchley!" After staring a moment and seeing their father look as strange, on his side, as Adela, though in a different way, the children also began to cry, so that when the servants arrived with tea and boiled eggs these functionaries were greatly embarrassed with their burden, not knowing whether to come in or hang back. They all scraped together a decorum, and as soon as the things had been put on table the Colonel banished the men with a glance. Then he made a little affectionate speech to Beatrice and Muriel, in which he described Mrs. Churchley as the kindest, the most delightful of women, only wanting to make them happy, only wanting to make *him* happy, and convinced that he would be if they were and that they would be if he was.

"What do such words mean?" Adela asked herself. She declared privately that they meant nothing, but she was silent, and every one was silent, on account of the advent of Miss Flynn the governess, before whom Colonel Chart preferred not to discuss the situation. Adela recognised on the spot that if things were to go as he wished his children would practically never again be alone with him. He would spend all his time with Mrs. Churchley till they were married, and then Mrs. Churchley would spend all her time with him. Adela was ashamed of him, and that was horrible—all the more that every one else would be, all his other friends, every one who had known her mother. But the public dishonour to that high memory shouldn't be enacted; he shouldn't do as he wished.

After breakfast her father remarked to her that it would give him pleasure if in a day or two she would take her sisters to see their friend, and she replied that he should be obeyed. He held her hand a moment, looking at her with an argument in his eyes which presently hardened into sternness. He wanted to know that she forgave him, but also wanted to assure her that he expected her to mind what she did, to go straight. She turned away her eyes; she was indeed ashamed of him.

She waited three days and then conveyed her sisters to the *repaire*, as she would have been ready to term it, of the lioness. That queen of beasts was surrounded with callers, as Adela knew she would be; it was her "day" and the occasion the girl preferred. Before this she had spent all her time with her companions, talking to them about their mother, playing on their memory of her, making them cry and making them laugh, reminding them of blest hours of their early childhood, telling them anecdotes of her own. None the less she confided to them that she believed there was no harm at all in Mrs. Churchley, and that when the time should come she would probably take them out immensely. She saw with smothered irritation that they enjoyed their visit at Prince's Gate; they had never been at anything so "grown-up," nor seen so many smart bonnets and brilliant complexions. Moreover they were considered with interest, quite as if, being minor elements, yet perceptible ones, of Mrs. Churchley's new life, they had been described in advance and were the heroines of the occasion. There were so many ladies present that this personage didn't talk to them much; she only called them her "chicks" and asked them to hand about tea-cups and bread and butter. All of which was highly agreeable and indeed intensely exciting to Beatrice and Muriel, who had little round red spots in *their* cheeks when they came away. Adela quivered with the sense that her mother's children were now Mrs. Churchley's "chicks" and a part of the furniture of Mrs. Churchley's dreadful consciousness.

It was one thing to have made up her mind, however; it was another thing to make her attempt. It was when she learned from Godfrey that the day was fixed, the 20th of July, only six weeks removed, that she felt the importance of prompt action. She learned everything from Godfrey now, having decided it would be hypocrisy to question her father. Even her silence was hypocritical, but she couldn't weep and wail. Her father showed extreme tact; taking no notice of her detachment, treating it as a moment of *bouderie* he was bound to allow her and that would pout itself away. She debated much as to whether she should take Godfrey into her confidence; she would have done so without hesitation if he hadn't disappointed her. He was so little what she might have expected, and so perversely preoccupied that she could explain it only by the high pressure at which he was living, his anxiety about his "exam." He was in a fidget, in a fever, putting on a spurt to come in first; sceptical moreover about his success and cynical about everything else. He appeared to agree to the general axiom that they didn't want a strange woman thrust into their life, but he found Mrs. Churchley "very jolly as a person to know." He had been to see her by himself—he had been to see her three times. He in fact gave it out that he would make the most of her now; he should probably be so little in Seymour Street after these days. What Adela at last determined to give him was her assurance that the marriage would never take place. When he asked what she meant and who was to prevent it she replied that the interesting couple would abandon the idea of themselves, or that Mrs. Churchley at least would after a week or two back out of it.

"That will be really horrid then," Godfrey pronounced. "The only respectable thing, at the point they've come to, is to put it through. Charming for poor Dad to have the air of being 'chucked'!"

This made her hesitate two days more, but she found answers more valid than any objections. The many-voiced answer to everything—it was like the autumn wind round the house—was the affront that fell back on her mother. Her mother was dead but it killed her again. So one morning at eleven o'clock, when she knew her father was writing letters, she went out quietly and, stopping the first hansom she met, drove to Prince's Gate. Mrs. Churchley was at home, and she was shown into the drawing-room with the request that she would wait five minutes. She waited without the sense of breaking down at the last, and the impulse to run away, which were what she had expected to have. In the cab and at the door her heart had beat terribly, but now suddenly, with the game really to play, she found herself lucid and calm. It was a joy to her to feel later that this was the way Mrs. Churchley found her: not confused, not stammering nor prevaricating, only a little amazed at her own courage, conscious of the immense responsibility of her step and wonderfully older than her years. Her hostess sounded her at first with suspicious eyes, but eventually, to Adela's surprise, burst into tears. At this the girl herself cried, and with the secret happiness of believing they were saved. Mrs. Churchley said she would think over what she had been told, and she promised her young friend, freely enough and very firmly, not to betray the secret of the latter's step to the Colonel. They were saved— they were saved: the words sung themselves in the girl's soul as she came downstairs. When the door opened for her she saw her brother on the step, and they looked at each other in surprise, each finding it on the part of the other an odd hour for Prince's Gate. Godfrey remarked that Mrs. Churchley would have enough of the family, and Adela answered that she would perhaps have too much. None the less the young man went in while his sister took her way home.

III

SHE saw nothing of him for nearly a week; he had more and more his own times and hours, adjusted to his tremendous responsibilities, and he spent whole days at his crammer's. When she knocked at his door late in the evening he was regularly not in his room. It was known in the house how much he was worried; he was horribly nervous about his ordeal. It was to begin on the 23rd of June, and his father was as worried as himself. The wedding had been arranged in relation to this; they wished poor Godfrey's fate settled first, though they felt the nuptials would be darkened if it shouldn't be settled right.

Ten days after that performance of her private undertaking Adela began to sniff, as it were, a difference in the general air; but as yet she was afraid to exult. It wasn't in truth a difference for the better, so that there might be still a great tension. Her father, since the announcement of his intended marriage, had been visibly pleased with himself, but that pleasure now appeared to have undergone a check. She had the impression known to the passengers on a great steamer when, in the middle of the night, they feel the engines stop. As this impression may easily sharpen to the sense that something serious has happened, so the girl asked herself what had actually occurred. She had expected something serious; but it was as if she couldn't keep still in her cabin—she wanted to go up and see. On the 20th, just before breakfast, her maid brought her a message from her brother. Mr. Godfrey would be obliged if she would speak to him in his room. She went straight up to him, dreading to find him ill, broken down on the eve of his formidable week. This was not the case however—he rather seemed already at work, to have been at work since dawn. But he was very white and his eyes had a strange and new expression. Her beautiful young brother looked older; he looked haggard and hard. He met her there as if he had been waiting for her, and he said at once: "Please tell me this, Adela—what was the purpose of your visit the other morning to Mrs. Churchley, the day I met you at her door?"

She stared—she cast about. "The purpose? What's the matter? Why do you ask?"

"They've put it off—they've put it off a month."

"Ah thank God!" said Adela.

"Why the devil do you thank God?" Godfrey asked with a strange impatience.

She gave a strained intense smile. "You know I think it all wrong."

He stood looking at her up and down. "What did you do there? How did you interfere?"

"Who told you I interfered?" she returned with a deep flush.

"You said something—you did something. I knew you had done it when I saw you come out."

"What I did was my own business."

"Damn your own business!" cried the young man.

She had never in her life been so spoken to, and in advance, had she been given the choice, would have said that she'd rather die than be so handled by Godfrey. But her spirit was high, and for a moment she was as angry as if she had been cut with a whip. She escaped the blow but felt the insult. "And *your* business then?" she asked. "I wondered what that was when I saw *you*."

He stood a moment longer scowling at her; then with the exclamation "You've made a pretty mess!" he turned away from her and sat down to his books.

They had put it off, as he said; her father was dry and stiff and official about it. "I suppose I had better let you know we've thought it best to postpone our marriage till the end of the summer—Mrs. Churchley has so many arrangements to make": he was not more expansive than that. She neither knew nor greatly cared whether she but vainly imagined or correctly observed him to watch her obliquely for some measure of her receipt of these words. She flattered herself that, thanks to Godfrey's forewarning, cruel as the form of it had been, she was able to repress any crude sign of elation. She had a perfectly good conscience, for she could now judge what odious elements Mrs. Churchley, whom she had not seen since the morning in Prince's Gate, had already introduced into their dealings. She gathered without difficulty that her father hadn't concurred in the postponement, for he was more restless than before, more absent and distinctly irritable. There was naturally still the question of how much of this condition was to be attributed to his solicitude about Godfrey. That young man took occasion to say a horrible thing to his sister: "If I don't pass it will be your fault." These were dreadful days for the girl, and she asked herself how she could have borne them if the hovering spirit of her mother hadn't been at her side. Fortunately she always felt it there, sustaining, commending, sanctifying. Suddenly her father announced to her that he wished her to go immediately, with her sisters, down to Brinton, where there was always part of a household and where for a few weeks they would manage well enough. The only explanation he gave of this desire was that he wanted them out of the way. "Out of the way of what?" she queried, since there were to be for the time no preparations in Seymour Street. She was willing to take it for out of the way of his nerves.

She never needed urging however to go to Brinton, the dearest old house in the world, where the happiest days of her young life had been spent and the silent nearness of her mother always seemed greatest. She was happy again, with Beatrice and Muriel and Miss Flynn, with the air of summer and the haunted rooms and her mother's garden and the talking oaks and the nightingales. She wrote briefly to her father, giving him, as he had requested, an account of things; and he wrote back that since she was so contented—she didn't recognise having told him that—she had better not return to town at all. The fag-end of the London season would be unimportant to her, and he was getting on very well. He mentioned that Godfrey had passed his tests, but, as she knew, there would be a tiresome wait before news of results. The poor chap was going abroad for a month with young Sherard—he had earned a little rest and a little fun. He went abroad without a word to Adela, but in his beautiful little hand he took a chaffing leave of Beatrice. The child showed her sister the letter, of which she was very proud and which contained no message for any one else. This was the worst bitterness of the whole crisis for that somebody—its placing in so strange a light the creature in the world whom, after her mother, she had loved best.

Colonel Chart had said he would "run down" while his children were at Brinton, but they heard no more about it. He only wrote two or three times to Miss Flynn on matters in regard to which Adela was surprised he shouldn't have communicated with herself. Muriel accomplished an upright little letter to Mrs. Churchley—her eldest sister neither fostered nor discouraged the performance—to which Mrs. Churchley replied, after a fortnight, in a meagre and, as Adela thought, illiterate fashion, making no allusion to the approach of any closer tie. Evidently the situation had changed; the question of the marriage was dropped, at any rate for the time. This idea gave our young woman a singular and almost intoxicating sense of power; she felt as if she were riding a great wave of confidence. She had decided and acted—the greatest could do no more than that. The grand thing was to see one's results, and what else was she doing? These results were in big rich conspicuous lives; the stage was large on which she moved her figures. Such a vision was exciting, and as they had the use of a couple of ponies at Brinton she worked off her excitement by a long gallop. A day or two after this however came news of which the effect was to rekindle it. Godfrey had come back, the list had been published, he had passed first. These happy tidings proceeded from the young man himself; he announced them by a telegram to Beatrice, who had never in her life before received such a missive and was proportionately inflated. Adela reflected that she herself ought to have felt snubbed, but she was too happy. They were free again, they were themselves, the nightmare of the previous weeks was blown away, the unity and dignity of her father's life restored, and, to round off her sense of success, Godfrey had achieved his first step toward high distinction. She wrote him the next day as frankly and affectionately as if there had been no estrangement between them, and besides telling him how she rejoiced in his triumph begged him in charity to let them know exactly how the case stood with regard to Mrs. Churchley.

Late in the summer afternoon she walked through the park to the village with her letter, posted it and came back. Suddenly, at one of the turns of the avenue, half-way to the house, she saw a young man hover there as if awaiting her—a young man who proved to be Godfrey on his pedestrian progress over from the station. He had seen her as he took his short cut, and if he had come down to Brinton it wasn't apparently to avoid her. There was nevertheless none of the joy of his triumph in his face as he came a very few steps to meet her; and although, stiffly enough, he let her kiss him and say "I'm so glad—I'm so glad!" she felt this tolerance as not quite the mere calm of the rising diplomatist. He turned toward the house with her and walked on a short distance while she uttered the hope that he had come to stay some days.

"Only till to-morrow morning. They're sending me straight to Madrid. I came down to say good-bye; there's a fellow bringing my bags."

"To Madrid? How awfully nice! And it's awfully nice of you to have come," she said as she passed her hand into his arm.

The movement made him stop, and, stopping, he turned on her in a flash a face of something more than, suspicion—of passionate reprobation. "What I really came for—you might as well know without more delay—is to ask you a question."

"A question?"—she echoed it with a beating heart.

They stood there under the old trees in the lingering light, and, young and fine and fair as they both were, formed a complete superficial harmony with the peaceful English scene. A near view, however, would have shown that Godfrey Chart hadn't taken so much trouble only to skim the surface. He looked deep into his sister's eyes. "What was it you said that morning to Mrs. Churchley?"

She fixed them on the ground a moment, but at last met his own again. "If she has told you, why do you ask?"

"She has told me nothing. I've seen for myself."

"What have you seen?"

"She has broken it off. Everything's over. Father's in the depths."

"In the depths?" the girl quavered.

"Did you think it would make him jolly?" he went on.

She had to choose what to say. "He'll get over it. He'll be glad."

"That remains to be seen. You interfered, you invented something, you got round her. I insist on knowing what you did."

Adela felt that if it was a question of obstinacy there was something within her she could count on; in spite of which, while she stood looking down again a moment, she said to herself "I could be dumb and dogged if I chose, but I scorn to be." She wasn't ashamed of what she had done, but she wanted to be clear. "Are you absolutely certain it's broken off?"

"He is, and she is; so that's as good."

"What reason has she given?"

"None at all—or half a dozen; it's the same thing. She has changed her mind—she mistook her feelings—she can't part with her independence. Moreover he has too many children."

"Did he tell you this?" the girl asked.

"Mrs. Churchley told me. She has gone abroad for a year."

"And she didn't tell you what I said to her?"

Godfrey showed an impatience. "Why should I take this trouble if she had?"

"You might have taken it to make me suffer," said Adela. "That appears to be what you want to do."

"No, I leave that to you—it's the good turn you've done me!" cried the young man with hot tears in his eyes.

She stared, aghast with the perception that there was some dreadful thing she didn't know; but he walked on, dropping the question angrily and turning his back to her as if he couldn't trust himself. She read his disgust in his averted, face, in the way he squared his shoulders and smote the ground with his stick, and she hurried after him and presently overtook him. She kept by him for a moment in silence; then she broke out: "What do you mean? What in the world have I done to you?"

"She would have helped me. She was all ready to help me," Godfrey portentously said.

"Helped you in what?" She wondered what he meant; if he had made debts that he was afraid to confess to his father and—of all horrible things— had been looking to Mrs. Churchley to pay. She turned red with the mere apprehension of this and, on the heels of her guess, exulted again at having perhaps averted such a shame.

"Can't you just see I'm in trouble? Where are your eyes, your senses, your sympathy, that you talk so much about? Haven't you seen these six months that I've a curst worry in my life?"

She seized his arm, made him stop, stood looking up at him like a frightened little girl. "What's the matter, Godfrey?—what *is* the matter?"

"You've gone against me so—I could strangle you!" he growled. This image added nothing to her dread; her dread was that he had done some wrong, was stained with some guilt. She uttered it to him with clasped hands, begging him to tell her the worst; but, still more passionately, he cut her short with his own cry: "In God's name, satisfy me! What infernal thing did you do?"

"It wasn't infernal—it was right. I told her mamma had been wretched," said Adela.

"Wretched? You told her such a lie?"

"It was the only way, and she believed me."

"Wretched how?—wretched when?—wretched where?" the young man stammered.

"I told her papa had made her so, and that *she* ought to know it. I told her the question troubled me unspeakably, but that I had made up my mind

31

it was my duty to initiate her." Adela paused, the light of bravado in her face, as if, though struck while the words came with the monstrosity of what she had done, she was incapable of abating a jot of it. "I notified her that he had faults and peculiarities that made mamma's life a long worry—a martyrdom that she hid wonderfully from the world, but that we saw and that I had often pitied. I told her what they were, these faults and peculiarities; I put the dots on the i's. I said it wasn't fair to let another person marry him without a warning. I warned her; I satisfied my conscience. She could do as she liked. My responsibility was over."

Godfrey gazed at her; he listened with parted lips, incredulous and appalled. "You invented such a tissue of falsities and calumnies, and you talk about your conscience? You stand there in your senses and proclaim your crime?"

"I'd have committed any crime that would have rescued us."

"You insult and blacken and ruin your own father?" Godfrey kept on.

"He'll never know it; she took a vow she wouldn't tell him."

"Ah I'll be damned if *I* won't tell him!" he rang out.

Adela felt sick at this, but she flamed up to resent the treachery, as it struck her, of such a menace. "I did right—I did right!" she vehemently declared "I went down on my knees to pray for guidance, and I saved mamma's memory from outrage. But if I hadn't, if I hadn't"—she faltered an instant—"I'm not worse than you, and I'm not so bad, for you've done something that you're ashamed to tell me."

He had taken out his watch; he looked at it with quick intensity, as if not hearing nor heeding her. Then, his calculating eyes raised, he fixed her long enough to exclaim with unsurpassable horror and contempt: "You raving maniac!" He turned away from her; he bounded down the avenue in the direction from which they had come, and, while she watched him, strode away, across the grass, toward the short cut to the station.

IV

His bags, by the time she got home, had been brought to the house, but Beatrice and Muriel, immediately informed of this, waited for their brother in vain. Their sister said nothing to them of her having seen him, and she accepted after a little, with a calmness that surprised herself, the idea that he had returned to town to denounce her. She believed this would make no difference now—she had done what she had done. She had somehow a stiff faith in Mrs. Churchley. Once that so considerable mass had received its impetus it wouldn't, it couldn't pull up. It represented a heavy-footed person, incapable of further agility. Adela recognised too how well it might have come over her that there were too many children. Lastly the girl fortified herself with the reflexion, grotesque in the conditions and conducing to prove her sense of humour not high, that her father was after all not a man to be played with. It seemed to her at any rate that if she *had* baffled his unholy purpose she could bear anything—bear imprisonment and bread and water, bear lashes and torture, bear even his lifelong reproach. What she could bear least was the wonder of the inconvenience she had inflicted on Godfrey. She had time to turn this over, very vainly, for a succession of days—days more numerous than she had expected, which passed without bringing her from London any summons to come up and take her punishment. She sounded the possible, she compared the degrees of the probable; feeling however that as a cloistered girl she was poorly equipped for speculation. She tried to imagine the calamitous things young men might do, and could only feel that such things would naturally be connected either with borrowed money or with bad women. She became conscious that after all she knew almost nothing about either of those interests. The worst woman she knew was Mrs. Churchley herself. Meanwhile there was no reverberation from Seymour Street—only a sultry silence.

At Brinton she spent hours in her mother's garden, where she had grown up, where she considered that she was training for old age, since she meant not to depend on whist. She loved the place as, had she been a good Catholic, she would have loved the smell of her parish church; and indeed there was in her passion for flowers something of the respect of a religion. They seemed to her the only things in the world that really respected themselves, unless one made an exception for Nutkins, who had been in command all through her mother's time, with whom she had had a real friendship and who had been affected by their pure example. He was the person left in the world with whom on the whole she could speak most intimately of the dead. They never had to name her together—they only said "she"; and Nutkins freely conceded that she had taught him everything he knew. When Beatrice and Muriel said "she" they referred to Mrs. Churchley. Adela had reason to believe she should never marry, and that some day she should have about a thousand a year. This made her see in the far future a little garden of her own, under a hill, full of rare and exquisite things, where she would spend most of her old age on her knees with an apron and stout gloves, with a pair of shears and a trowel, steeped in the comfort of being thought mad.

One morning ten days after her scene with Godfrey, on coming back into the house shortly before lunch, she was met by Miss Flynn with the notification that a lady in the drawing-room had been waiting for her for some minutes. "A lady" suggested immediately Mrs. Churchley. It came over Adela that the form in which her penalty was to descend would be a personal explanation with that misdirected woman. The lady had given no name, and Miss Flynn hadn't seen Mrs. Churchley; nevertheless the governess was certain Adela's surmise was wrong.

"Is she big and dreadful?" the girl asked.

Miss Flynn, who was circumspection itself, took her time. "She's dreadful, but she's not big." She added that she wasn't sure she ought to let Adela go in alone; but this young lady took herself throughout for a heroine, and it wasn't in a heroine to shrink from any encounter. Wasn't she every instant in transcendent contact with her mother? The visitor might have no connexion whatever with the drama of her father's frustrated marriage; but everything to-day for Adela was part of that.

Miss Flynn's description had prepared her for a considerable shock, but she wasn't agitated by her first glimpse of the person who awaited her. A youngish well-dressed woman stood there, and silence was between them while they looked at each other. Before either had spoken however Adela began to see what Miss Flynn had intended. In the light of the drawing-room window the lady was five-and-thirty years of age and had vivid yellow hair. She also had a blue cloth suit with brass buttons, a stick-up collar like a gentleman's, a necktie arranged in a sailor's knot, a golden pin in the shape of a little lawn-tennis racket, and pearl-grey gloves with big black stitchings. Adela's second impression was that she was an actress, and her third that no such person had ever before crossed that threshold.

"I'll tell you what I've come for," said the apparition. "I've come to ask you to intercede." She wasn't an actress; an actress would have had a nicer voice.

"To intercede?" Adela was too bewildered to ask her to sit down.

"With your father, you know. He doesn't know, but he'll have to." Her "have" sounded like "'ave." She explained, with many more such sounds, that she was Mrs. Godfrey, that they had been married seven mortal months. If Godfrey was going abroad she must go with him, and the only way she could go with him would be for his father to do something. He was afraid of his father—that was clear; he was afraid even to tell him. What she had come down for was to see some other member of the family face to face—"fice to fice," Mrs. Godfrey called it—and try if he couldn't be approached by another side. If no one else would act then she would just have to act herself. The Colonel would have to do something—that was the only way out of it.

What really happened Adela never quite understood; what seemed to be happening was that the room went round and round. Through the blur of perception accompanying this effect the sharp stabs of her visitor's revelation came to her like the words heard by a patient "going off" under ether. She afterwards denied passionately even to herself that she had done anything so abject as to faint; but there was a lapse in her consciousness on the score of Miss Flynn's intervention. This intervention had evidently been active, for when they talked the matter over, later in the day, with bated breath and infinite dissimulation for the school-room quarter, the governess had more lurid truths, and still more, to impart than to receive. She was at any rate under the impression that she had athletically contended, in the drawing-room, with the yellow hair—this after removing Adela from the scene and before inducing Mrs. Godfrey to withdraw. Miss Flynn had never known a more thrilling day, for all the rest of it too was pervaded with agitations and conversations, precautions and alarms. It was given out to Beatrice and Muriel that their sister had been taken suddenly ill, and the governess ministered to her in her room. Indeed Adela had never found herself less at ease, for this time she had received a blow that she couldn't return. There was nothing to do but to take it, to endure the humiliation of her wound.

At first she declined to take it—having, as might appear, the much more attractive resource of regarding her visitant as a mere masquerading person, an impudent impostor. On the face of the matter moreover it wasn't fair to believe till one heard; and to hear in such a case was to hear Godfrey himself. Whatever she had tried to imagine about him she hadn't arrived at anything so belittling as an idiotic secret marriage with a dyed and painted hag. Adela repeated this last word as if it gave her comfort; and indeed where everything was so bad fifteen years of seniority made the case little worse. Miss Flynn was portentous, for Miss Flynn had had it out with the wretch. She had cross-questioned her and had not broken her down. This was the most uplifted hour of Miss Flynn's life; for whereas she usually had to content herself with being humbly and gloomily in the right she could now be magnanimously and showily so. Her only perplexity was as to what she ought to do—write to Colonel Chart or go up to town to see him. She bloomed with alternatives—she resembled some dull garden-path which under a copious downpour has begun to flaunt with colour. Toward evening Adela was obliged to recognise that her brother's worry, of which he had spoken to her, had appeared bad enough to consist even of a low wife, and to remember that, so far from its being inconceivable a young man in his position should clandestinely take one, she had been present, years before, during her mother's lifetime, when Lady Molesley declared gaily, over a cup of tea, that this was precisely what she expected of her eldest son. The next morning it was the worst possibilities that seemed clearest; the only thing left with a tatter of dusky comfort being the ambiguity of Godfrey's charge that her own action had "done" for him.

That was a matter by itself, and she racked her brains for a connecting link between Mrs. Churchley and Mrs. Godfrey. At last she made up her mind that they were related by blood; very likely, though differing in fortune, they were cousins or even sisters. But even then what did the wretched boy mean?

Arrested by the unnatural fascination of opportunity, Miss Flynn received before lunch a telegram from Colonel Chart—an order for dinner and a vehicle; he and Godfrey were to arrive at six o'clock. Adela had plenty of occupation for the interval, since she was pitying her father when she wasn't rejoicing that her mother had gone too soon to know. She flattered herself she made out the providential reason of that cruelty now. She found time however still to wonder for what purpose, given the situation, Godfrey was to be brought down. She wasn't unconscious indeed that she had little general knowledge of what usually was done with young men in that predicament. One talked about the situation, but the situation was an abyss. She felt this still more when she found, on her father's arrival, that nothing apparently was to happen as she had taken for granted it would. There was an inviolable hush over the whole affair, but no tragedy, no publicity, nothing ugly. The tragedy had been in town—the faces of the two men spoke of it in spite of their other perfunctory aspects; and at present there was only a family dinner, with Beatrice and Muriel and the governess—with almost a company tone too, the result of the desire to avoid publicity. Adela admired her father; she knew what he was feeling if Mrs. Godfrey had been at him, and yet she saw him positively gallant. He was mildly austere, or rather even—what was it?—august; just as, coldly equivocal, he never looked at his son, so that at moments he struck her as almost sick with sadness. Godfrey was equally inscrutable and therefore wholly different from what he had been as he stood before her in the park. If he was to start on his career (with such a wife!—wouldn't she utterly blight it?) he was already professional enough to know how to wear a mask.

Before they rose from table she felt herself wholly bewildered, so little were such large causes traceable in their effects. She had nerved herself for a great ordeal, but the air was as sweet as an anodyne. It was perfectly plain to her that her father was deadly sore—as pathetic as a person betrayed. He was broken, but he showed no resentment; there was a weight on his heart, but he had lightened it by dressing as immaculately as usual for dinner. She asked herself what immensity of a row there could have been in town to have left his anger so spent. He went through everything, even to sitting with his son after dinner. When they came out together he invited Beatrice and Muriel to the billiard-room, and as Miss Flynn discreetly withdrew Adela was left alone with Godfrey, who was completely changed and not now in the least of a rage. He was broken too, but not so pathetic as his father. He was only very correct and apologetic he said to his sister: "I'm awfully sorry *you* were annoyed—it was something I never dreamed of."

She couldn't think immediately what he meant; then she grasped the reference to her extraordinary invader. She was uncertain, however, what tone to take; perhaps his father had arranged with him that they were to make the best of it. But she spoke her own despair in the way she murmured "Oh Godfrey, Godfrey, is it true?"

"I've been the most unutterable donkey—you can say what you like to me. You can't say anything worse than I've said to myself."

"My brother, my brother!"—his words made her wail it out. He hushed her with a movement and she asked: "What has father said?"

He looked very high over her head. "He'll give her six hundred a year."

"Ah the angel!"—it was too splendid.

"On condition"—Godfrey scarce blinked—"she never comes near me. She has solemnly promised, and she'll probably leave me alone to get the money. If she doesn't—in diplomacy—I'm lost." He had been turning his eyes vaguely about, this way and that, to avoid meeting hers; but after another instant he gave up the effort and she had the miserable confession of his glance. "I've been living in hell."

"My brother, my brother!" she yearningly repeated.

"I'm not an idiot; yet for her I've behaved like one. Don't ask me—you mustn't know. It was all done in a day, and since then fancy my condition; fancy my work in such a torment; fancy my coming through at all."

"Thank God you passed!" she cried. "You were wonderful!"

"I'd have shot myself if I hadn't been. I had an awful day yesterday with the governor; it was late at night before it was over. I leave England next week. He brought me down here for it to look well—so that the children shan't know."

"*He's* wonderful too!" Adela murmured.

"Wonderful too!" Godfrey echoed.

"Did *she* tell him?" the girl went on.

"She came straight to Seymour Street from here. She saw him alone first; then he called me in. *That* luxury lasted about an hour."

"Poor, poor father!" Adela moaned at this; on which her brother remained silent. Then after he had alluded to it as the scene he had lived in terror of all through his cramming, and she had sighed forth again her pity and admiration for such a mixture of anxieties and such a triumph of talent, she pursued: "Have you told him?"

"Told him what?"

"What you said you would—what *I* did."

Godfrey turned away as if at present he had very little interest in that inferior tribulation. "I was angry with you, but I cooled off. I held my tongue."

She clasped her hands. "You thought of mamma!"

"Oh don't speak of mamma!" he cried as in rueful tenderness.

It was indeed not a happy moment, and she murmured: "No; if you *had* thought of her—!"

This made Godfrey face her again with a small flare in his eyes. "Oh *then* it didn't prevent. I thought that woman really good. I believed in her."

"Is she *very* bad?"

"I shall never mention her to you again," he returned with dignity.

"You may believe *I* won't speak of her! So father doesn't know?" the girl added.

"Doesn't know what?"

"That I said what I did to Mrs. Churchley."

He had a momentary pause. "I don't think so, but you must find out for yourself."

"I shall find out," said Adela. "But what had Mrs. Churchley to do with it?"

"With *my* misery? I told her. I had to tell some one."

"Why didn't you tell me?"

He appeared—though but after an instant—to know exactly why. "Oh you take things so beastly hard—you make such rows." Adela covered her face with her hands and he went on: "What I wanted was comfort—not to be lashed up. I thought I should go mad. I wanted Mrs. Churchley to break it to father, to intercede for me and help him to meet it. She was awfully kind to me, she listened and she understood; she could fancy how it had happened. Without her I shouldn't have pulled through. She liked me, you know," he further explained, and as if it were quite worth mentioning—all the more that it was pleasant to him. "She said she'd do what she could for me. She was full of sympathy and resource. I really leaned on her. But when *you* cut in of course it spoiled everything. That's why I was so furious with you. She couldn't do anything then."

Adela dropped her hands, staring; she felt she had walked in darkness. "So that he had to meet it alone?"

"*Dame!*" said Godfrey, who had got up his French tremendously.

Muriel came to the door to say papa wished the two others to join them, and the next day Godfrey returned to town. His father remained at

Brinton, without an intermission, the rest of the summer and the whole of the autumn, and Adela had a chance to find out, as she had said, whether he knew she had interfered. But in spite of her chance she never found out. He knew Mrs. Churchley had thrown him over and he knew his daughter rejoiced in it, but he appeared not to have divined the relation between the two facts. It was strange that one of the matters he was clearest about— Adela's secret triumph—should have been just the thing which from this time on justified less and less such a confidence. She was too sorry for him to be consistently glad. She watched his attempts to wind himself up on the subject of shorthorns and drainage, and she favoured to the utmost of her ability his intermittent disposition to make a figure in orchids. She wondered whether they mightn't have a few people at Brinton; but when she mentioned the idea he asked what in the world there would be to attract them. It was a confoundedly stupid house, he remarked—with all respect to *her* cleverness. Beatrice and Muriel were mystified; the prospect of going out immensely had faded so utterly away. They were apparently not to go out at all. Colonel Chart was aimless and bored; he paced up and down and went back to smoking, which was bad for him, and looked drearily out of windows as if on the bare chance that something might arrive. Did he expect Mrs. Churchley to arrive, did he expect her to relent on finding she couldn't live without him? It was Adela's belief that she gave no sign. But the girl thought it really remarkable of her not to have betrayed her ingenious young visitor. Adela's judgement of human nature was perhaps harsh, but she believed that most women, given the various facts, wouldn't have been so forbearing. This lady's conception of the point of honour placed her there in a finer and purer light than had at all originally promised to shine about her.

She meanwhile herself could well judge how heavy her father found the burden of Godfrey's folly and how he was incommoded at having to pay the horrible woman six hundred a year. Doubtless he was having dreadful letters from her; doubtless she threatened them all with hideous exposure. If the matter should be bruited Godfrey's prospects would collapse on the spot. He thought Madrid very charming and curious, but Mrs. Godfrey was in England, so that his father had to face the music. Adela took a dolorous comfort in her mother's being out of that—it would have killed her; but this

41

didn't blind her to the fact that the comfort for her father would perhaps have been greater if he had had some one to talk to about his trouble. He never dreamed of doing so to her, and she felt she couldn't ask him. In the family life he wanted utter silence about it. Early in the winter he went abroad for ten weeks, leaving her with her sisters in the country, where it was not to be denied that at this time existence had very little savour. She half expected her sister-in-law would again descend on her; but the fear wasn't justified, and the quietude of the awful creature seemed really to vibrate with the ring of gold-pieces. There were sure to be extras. Adela winced at the extras. Colonel Chart went to Paris and to Monte Carlo and then to Madrid to see his boy. His daughter had the vision of his perhaps meeting Mrs. Churchley somewhere, since, if she had gone for a year, she would still be on the Continent. If he should meet her perhaps the affair would come on again: she caught herself musing over this. But he brought back no such appearance, and, seeing him after an interval, she was struck afresh with his jilted and wasted air. She didn't like it—she resented it. A little more and she would have said that that was no way to treat so faithful a man.

They all went up to town in March, and on one of the first days of April she saw Mrs. Churchley in the Park. She herself remained apparently invisible to that lady—she herself and Beatrice and Muriel, who sat with her in their mother's old bottle-green landau. Mrs. Churchley, perched higher than ever, rode by without a recognition; but this didn't prevent Adela's going to her before the month was over. As on her great previous occasion she went in the morning, and she again had the good fortune to be admitted. This time, however, her visit was shorter, and a week after making it—the week was a desolation—she addressed to her brother at Madrid a letter containing these words: "I could endure it no longer—I confessed and retracted; I explained to her as well as I could the falsity of what I said to her ten months ago and the benighted purity of my motives for saying it. I besought her to regard it as unsaid, to forgive me, not to despise me too much, to take pity on poor *perfect* papa and come back to him. She was more good-natured than you might have expected—indeed she laughed extravagantly. She had never believed me—it was too absurd; she had only, at the time, disliked me. She found me utterly false—she was very frank with me about this—and she told papa she really thought me horrid. She said she could never live with such a girl, and as I would certainly never marry I must be sent away—in short she quite loathed me. Papa defended me, he refused to sacrifice me, and this led practically to their rupture. Papa gave her up, as it were, for *me*. Fancy the angel, and fancy what I must try to be to him for the rest of his life! Mrs. Churchley can never come back—she's going to marry Lord Dovedale."

About Author

Henry James OM (15 April 1843 – 28 February 1916) was an American-British author regarded as a key transitional figure between literary realism and literary modernism, and is considered by many to be among the greatest novelists in the English language. He was the son of Henry James Sr. and the brother of renowned philosopher and psychologist William James and diarist Alice James.

He is best known for a number of novels dealing with the social and marital interplay between émigré Americans, English people, and continental Europeans. Examples of such novels include The Portrait of a Lady, The Ambassadors, and The Wings of the Dove. His later works were increasingly experimental. In describing the internal states of mind and social dynamics of his characters, James often made use of a style in which ambiguous or contradictory motives and impressions were overlaid or juxtaposed in the discussion of a character's psyche. For their unique ambiguity, as well as for other aspects of their composition, his late works have been compared to impressionist painting.

His novella The Turn of the Screw has garnered a reputation as the most analysed and ambiguous ghost story in the English language and remains his most widely adapted work in other media. He also wrote a number of other highly regarded ghost stories and is considered one of the greatest masters of the field.

James published articles and books of criticism, travel, biography, autobiography, and plays. Born in the United States, James largely relocated to Europe as a young man and eventually settled in England, becoming a British subject in 1915, one year before his death. James was nominated for the Nobel Prize in Literature in 1911, 1912 and 1916.

Life

Early years, 1843–1883

James was born at 2 Washington Place in New York City on 15 April 1843. His parents were Mary Walsh and Henry James Sr. His father was intelligent and steadfastly congenial. He was a lecturer and philosopher who had inherited independent means from his father, an Albany banker and investor. Mary came from a wealthy family long settled in New York City. Her sister Katherine lived with her adult family for an extended period of time. Henry Jr. had three brothers, William, who was one year his senior, and younger brothers Wilkinson (Wilkie) and Robertson. His younger sister was Alice. Both of his parents were of Irish and Scottish descent.

The family first lived in Albany, at 70 N. Pearl St., and then moved to Fourteenth Street in New York City when James was still a young boy. His education was calculated by his father to expose him to many influences, primarily scientific and philosophical; it was described by Percy Lubbock, the editor of his selected letters, as "extraordinarily haphazard and promiscuous." James did not share the usual education in Latin and Greek classics. Between 1855 and 1860, the James' household traveled to London, Paris, Geneva, Boulogne-sur-Mer and Newport, Rhode Island, according to the father's current interests and publishing ventures, retreating to the United States when funds were low. Henry studied primarily with tutors and briefly attended schools while the family traveled in Europe. Their longest stays were in France, where Henry began to feel at home and became fluent in French. He was afflicted with a stutter, which seems to have manifested itself only when he spoke English; in French, he did not stutter.

In 1860 the family returned to Newport. There Henry became a friend of the painter John La Farge, who introduced him to French literature, and in particular, to Balzac. James later called Balzac his "greatest master," and said that he had learned more about the craft of fiction from him than from anyone else.

In the autumn of 1861 Henry received an injury, probably to his back, while fighting a fire. This injury, which resurfaced at times throughout his life, made him unfit for military service in the American Civil War.

In 1864 the James family moved to Boston, Massachusetts to be near William, who had enrolled first in the Lawrence Scientific School at Harvard and then in the medical school. In 1862 Henry attended Harvard Law School, but realised that he was not interested in studying law. He pursued his interest in literature and associated with authors and critics William Dean Howells and Charles Eliot Norton in Boston and Cambridge, formed lifelong friendships with Oliver Wendell Holmes Jr., the future Supreme Court Justice, and with James and Annie Fields, his first professional mentors.

His first published work was a review of a stage performance, "Miss Maggie Mitchell in Fanchon the Cricket," published in 1863. About a year later, A Tragedy of Error, his first short story, was published anonymously. James's first payment was for an appreciation of Sir Walter Scott's novels, written for the North American Review. He wrote fiction and non-fiction pieces for The Nation and Atlantic Monthly, where Fields was editor. In 1871 he published his first novel, Watch and Ward, in serial form in the Atlantic Monthly. The novel was later published in book form in 1878.

During a 14-month trip through Europe in 1869–70 he met Ruskin, Dickens, Matthew Arnold, William Morris, and George Eliot. Rome impressed him profoundly. "Here I am then in the Eternal City," he wrote to his brother William. "At last—for the first time—I live!" He attempted to support himself as a freelance writer in Rome, then secured a position as Paris correspondent for the New York Tribune, through the influence of its editor John Hay. When these efforts failed he returned to New York City. During 1874 and 1875 he published Transatlantic Sketches, A Passionate Pilgrim, and Roderick Hudson. During this early period in his career he was influenced by Nathaniel Hawthorne.

In 1869 he settled in London. There he established relationships with Macmillan and other publishers, who paid for serial installments that they would later publish in book form. The audience for these serialized novels was largely made up of middle-class women, and James struggled to fashion serious literary work within the strictures imposed by editors' and publishers' notions of what was suitable for young women to read. He lived in rented rooms but was able to join gentlemen's clubs that had libraries and where he could entertain male friends. He was introduced to English society by Henry Adams and Charles Milnes Gaskell, the latter introducing him to the Travellers' and the Reform Clubs.

In the fall of 1875 he moved to the Latin Quarter of Paris. Aside from two trips to America, he spent the next three decades—the rest of his life—in Europe. In Paris he met Zola, Alphonse Daudet, Maupassant, Turgenev, and others. He stayed in Paris only a year before moving to London.

In England he met the leading figures of politics and culture. He continued to be a prolific writer, producing The American (1877), The Europeans (1878), a revision of Watch and Ward (1878), French Poets and Novelists (1878), Hawthorne (1879), and several shorter works of fiction. In 1878 Daisy Miller established his fame on both sides of the Atlantic. It drew notice perhaps mostly because it depicted a woman whose behavior is outside the social norms of Europe. He also began his first masterpiece, The Portrait of a Lady, which would appear in 1881.

In 1877 he first visited Wenlock Abbey in Shropshire, home of his friend Charles Milnes Gaskell whom he had met through Henry Adams. He was much inspired by the darkly romantic Abbey and the surrounding countryside, which features in his essay Abbeys and Castles. In particular the gloomy monastic fishponds behind the Abbey are said to have inspired the lake in The Turn of the Screw.

While living in London, James continued to follow the careers of the "French realists", Émile Zola in particular. Their stylistic methods influenced his own work in the years to come. Hawthorne's influence on him faded during this period, replaced by George Eliot and Ivan Turgenev. 1879–1882 saw the publication of The Europeans, Washington Square, Confidence, and The Portrait of a Lady. He visited America in 1882–1883, then returned to London.

The period from 1881 to 1883 was marked by several losses. His mother died in 1881, followed by his father a few months later, and then by his brother Wilkie. Emerson, an old family friend, died in 1882. His friend Turgenev died in 1883.

Middle years, 1884–1897

In 1884 James made another visit to Paris. There he met again with Zola, Daudet, and Goncourt. He had been following the careers of the French "realist" or "naturalist" writers, and was increasingly influenced by them. In 1886, he published The Bostonians and The Princess Casamassima, both influenced by the French writers he'd studied assiduously. Critical reaction and sales were poor. He wrote to Howells that the books had hurt his career rather than helped because they had "reduced the desire, and demand, for my productions to zero". During this time he became friends with Robert Louis Stevenson, John Singer Sargent, Edmund Gosse, George du Maurier, Paul Bourget, and Constance Fenimore Woolson. His third novel from the 1880s was The Tragic Muse. Although he was following the precepts of Zola in his novels of the '80s, their tone and attitude are closer to the fiction of Alphonse Daudet. The lack of critical and financial success for his novels during this period led him to try writing for the theatre. (His dramatic works and his experiences with theatre are discussed below.)

In the last quarter of 1889, he started translating "for pure and copious lucre" Port Tarascon, the third volume of Alphonse Daudet adventures of Tartarin de Tarascon. Serialized in Harper's Monthly Magazine from June 1890, this translation praised as "clever" by The Spectator was published in January 1891 by Sampson Low, Marston, Searle & Rivington.

After the stage failure of Guy Domville in 1895, James was near despair and thoughts of death plagued him. The years spent on dramatic works were not entirely a loss. As he moved into the last phase of his career he found ways to adapt dramatic techniques into the novel form.

In the late 1880s and throughout the 1890s James made several trips through Europe. He spent a long stay in Italy in 1887. In that year the short novel The Aspern Papers and The Reverberator were published.

Late years, 1898–1916

In 1897–1898 he moved to Rye, Sussex, and wrote The Turn of the Screw. 1899–1900 saw the publication of The Awkward Age and The Sacred

Fount. During 1902–1904 he wrote The Ambassadors, The Wings of the Dove, and The Golden Bowl.

In 1904 he revisited America and lectured on Balzac. In 1906–1910 he published The American Scene and edited the "New York Edition", a 24-volume collection of his works. In 1910 his brother William died; Henry had just joined William from an unsuccessful search for relief in Europe on what then turned out to be his (Henry's) last visit to the United States (from summer 1910 to July 1911), and was near him, according to a letter he wrote, when he died.

In 1913 he wrote his autobiographies, A Small Boy and Others, and Notes of a Son and Brother. After the outbreak of the First World War in 1914 he did war work. In 1915 he became a British subject and was awarded the Order of Merit the following year. He died on 28 February 1916, in Chelsea, London. As he requested, his ashes were buried in Cambridge Cemetery in Massachusetts.

Biographers

James regularly rejected suggestions that he should marry, and after settling in London proclaimed himself "a bachelor". F. W. Dupee, in several volumes on the James family, originated the theory that he had been in love with his cousin Mary ("Minnie") Temple, but that a neurotic fear of sex kept him from admitting such affections: "James's invalidism ... was itself the symptom of some fear of or scruple against sexual love on his part." Dupee used an episode from James's memoir A Small Boy and Others, recounting a dream of a Napoleonic image in the Louvre, to exemplify James's romanticism about Europe, a Napoleonic fantasy into which he fled.

Dupee had not had access to the James family papers and worked principally from James's published memoir of his older brother, William, and the limited collection of letters edited by Percy Lubbock, heavily weighted toward James's last years. His account therefore moved directly from James's childhood, when he trailed after his older brother, to elderly invalidism. As more material became available to scholars, including the diaries of contemporaries and hundreds of affectionate and sometimes erotic letters written by James to younger men, the picture of neurotic celibacy gave way to a portrait of a closeted homosexual.

Between 1953 and 1972, Leon Edel authored a major five-volume biography of James, which accessed unpublished letters and documents after Edel gained the permission of James's family. Edel's portrayal of James included the suggestion he was celibate. It was a view first propounded by critic Saul Rosenzweig in 1943. In 1996 Sheldon M. Novick published Henry James: The Young Master, followed by Henry James: The Mature Master (2007). The first book "caused something of an uproar in Jamesian circles" as it challenged the previous received notion of celibacy, a once-familiar paradigm in biographies of homosexuals when direct evidence was non-existent. Novick also criticised Edel for following the discounted Freudian interpretation of homosexuality "as a kind of failure." The difference of opinion erupted in a series of exchanges between Edel and Novick which were published by the online magazine Slate, with the latter arguing that even the suggestion of celibacy went against James's own injunction "live!"—not "fantasize!"

A letter James wrote in old age to Hugh Walpole has been cited as an explicit statement of this. Walpole confessed to him of indulging in "high jinks", and James wrote a reply endorsing it: "We must know, as much as possible, in our beautiful art, yours & mine, what we are talking about — & the only way to know it is to have lived & loved & cursed & floundered & enjoyed & suffered — I don't think I regret a single 'excess' of my responsive youth".

The interpretation of James as living a less austere emotional life has been subsequently explored by other scholars. The often intense politics of Jamesian scholarship has also been the subject of studies. Author Colm Tóibín has said that Eve Kosofsky Sedgwick's Epistemology of the Closet made a landmark difference to Jamesian scholarship by arguing that he be read as a homosexual writer whose desire to keep his sexuality a secret shaped his layered style and dramatic artistry. According to Tóibín such a reading "removed James from the realm of dead white males who wrote about posh people. He became our contemporary."

51

James's letters to expatriate American sculptor Hendrik Christian Andersen have attracted particular attention. James met the 27-year-old Andersen in Rome in 1899, when James was 56, and wrote letters to Andersen that are intensely emotional: "I hold you, dearest boy, in my innermost love, & count on your feeling me—in every throb of your soul". In a letter of 6 May 1904, to his brother William, James referred to himself as "always your hopelessly celibate even though sexagenarian Henry". How accurate that description might have been is the subject of contention among James's biographers, but the letters to Andersen were occasionally quasi-erotic: "I put, my dear boy, my arm around you, & feel the pulsation, thereby, as it were, of our excellent future & your admirable endowment." To his homosexual friend Howard Sturgis, James could write: "I repeat, almost to indiscretion, that I could live with you. Meanwhile I can only try to live without you."

His numerous letters to the many young gay men among his close male friends are more forthcoming. In a letter to Howard Sturgis, following a long visit, James refers jocularly to their "happy little congress of two" and in letters to Hugh Walpole he pursues convoluted jokes and puns about their relationship, referring to himself as an elephant who "paws you oh so benevolently" and winds about Walpole his "well meaning old trunk". His letters to Walter Berry printed by the Black Sun Press have long been celebrated for their lightly veiled eroticism.

He corresponded in almost equally extravagant language with his many female friends, writing, for example, to fellow novelist Lucy Clifford: "Dearest Lucy! What shall I say? when I love you so very, very much, and see you nine times for once that I see Others! Therefore I think that—if you want it made clear to the meanest intelligence—I love you more than I love Others." To his New York friend Mary Cadwalader Jones: "Dearest Mary Cadwalader. I yearn over you, but I yearn in vain; & your long silence really breaks my heart, mystifies, depresses, almost alarms me, to the point even of making me wonder if poor unconscious & doting old Célimare [Jones's pet name for James] has 'done' anything, in some dark somnambulism of the spirit, which has ... given you a bad moment, or a wrong impression, or a 'colourable pretext' ... However these things may be, he loves you as tenderly as ever;

nothing, to the end of time, will ever detach him from you, & he remembers those Eleventh St. matutinal intimes hours, those telephonic matinées, as the most romantic of his life ..." His long friendship with American novelist Constance Fenimore Woolson, in whose house he lived for a number of weeks in Italy in 1887, and his shock and grief over her suicide in 1894, are discussed in detail in Edel's biography and play a central role in a study by Lyndall Gordon. (Edel conjectured that Woolson was in love with James and killed herself in part because of his coldness, but Woolson's biographers have objected to Edel's account.)

Works

Style and themes

James is one of the major figures of trans-Atlantic literature. His works frequently juxtapose characters from the Old World (Europe), embodying a feudal civilisation that is beautiful, often corrupt, and alluring, and from the New World (United States), where people are often brash, open, and assertive and embody the virtues—freedom and a more highly evolved moral character—of the new American society. James explores this clash of personalities and cultures, in stories of personal relationships in which power is exercised well or badly. His protagonists were often young American women facing oppression or abuse, and as his secretary Theodora Bosanquet remarked in her monograph Henry James at Work:

> When he walked out of the refuge of his study and into the world and looked around him, he saw a place of torment, where creatures of prey perpetually thrust their claws into the quivering flesh of doomed, defenseless children of light ... His novels are a repeated exposure of this wickedness, a reiterated and passionate plea for the fullest freedom of development, unimperiled by reckless and barbarous stupidity.

Critics have jokingly described three phases in the development of James's prose: "James I, James II, and The Old Pretender." He wrote short stories and plays. Finally, in his third and last period he returned to the long, serialised novel. Beginning in the second period, but most noticeably in the third, he increasingly abandoned direct statement in favour of frequent double negatives, and complex descriptive imagery. Single paragraphs began to run for page after page, in which an initial noun would be succeeded by pronouns surrounded by clouds of adjectives and prepositional clauses, far from their original referents, and verbs would be deferred and then preceded by a series of adverbs. The overall effect could be a vivid evocation of a scene as perceived by a sensitive observer. It has been debated whether this change of style was engendered by James's shifting from writing to dictating to a typist, a change made during the composition of What Maisie Knew.

In its intense focus on the consciousness of his major characters, James's later work foreshadows extensive developments in 20th century fiction. Indeed, he might have influenced stream-of-consciousness writers such as Virginia Woolf, who not only read some of his novels but also wrote essays about them. Both contemporary and modern readers have found the late style difficult and unnecessary; his friend Edith Wharton, who admired him greatly, said that there were passages in his work that were all but incomprehensible. James was harshly portrayed by H. G. Wells as a hippopotamus laboriously attempting to pick up a pea that had got into a corner of its cage. The "late James" style was ably parodied by Max Beerbohm in "The Mote in the Middle Distance".

More important for his work overall may have been his position as an expatriate, and in other ways an outsider, living in Europe. While he came from middle-class and provincial beginnings (seen from the perspective of European polite society) he worked very hard to gain access to all levels of society, and the settings of his fiction range from working class to aristocratic, and often describe the efforts of middle-class Americans to make their way in European capitals. He confessed he got some of his best story ideas from gossip at the dinner table or at country house weekends. He worked for a living, however, and lacked the experiences of select schools, university, and army service, the common bonds of masculine society. He was furthermore a man whose tastes and interests were, according to the prevailing standards of Victorian era Anglo-American culture, rather feminine, and who was shadowed by the cloud of prejudice that then and later accompanied suspicions of his homosexuality. Edmund Wilson famously compared James's objectivity to Shakespeare's:

54

One would be in a position to appreciate James better if one compared him with the dramatists of the seventeenth century—Racine and Molière, whom he resembles in form as well as in point of view, and even Shakespeare, when allowances are made for the most extreme differences in subject and form. These poets are not, like Dickens and Hardy, writers of melodrama—either humorous or pessimistic, nor secretaries of society like Balzac, nor prophets like Tolstoy: they are occupied simply with the presentation of conflicts of moral character, which they do not concern themselves about softening or averting. They do not indict society for these situations: they regard them as universal and inevitable. They do not even blame God for allowing them: they accept them as the conditions of life.

It is also possible to see many of James's stories as psychological thought-experiments. In his preface to the New York edition of The American he describes the development of the story in his mind as exactly such: the "situation" of an American, "some robust but insidiously beguiled and betrayed, some cruelly wronged, compatriot..." with the focus of the story being on the response of this wronged man. The Portrait of a Lady may be an experiment to see what happens when an idealistic young woman suddenly becomes very rich. In many of his tales, characters seem to exemplify alternative futures and possibilities, as most markedly in "The Jolly Corner", in which the protagonist and a ghost-doppelganger live alternative American and European lives; and in others, like The Ambassadors, an older James seems fondly to regard his own younger self facing a crucial moment.

Major novels

The first period of James's fiction, usually considered to have culminated in The Portrait of a Lady, concentrated on the contrast between Europe and America. The style of these novels is generally straightforward and, though personally characteristic, well within the norms of 19th-century fiction. Roderick Hudson (1875) is a Künstlerroman that traces the development of the title character, an extremely talented sculptor. Although the book shows some signs of immaturity—this was James's first serious attempt at a full-length novel—it has attracted favourable comment due to the vivid realisation of the three major characters: Roderick Hudson, superbly gifted but unstable and unreliable; Rowland Mallet, Roderick's limited but much more mature friend and patron; and Christina Light, one of James's most enchanting and maddening femmes fatales. The pair of Hudson and Mallet has been seen as representing the two sides of James's own nature: the wildly imaginative artist and the brooding conscientious mentor.

In The Portrait of a Lady (1881) James concluded the first phase of his career with a novel that remains his most popular piece of long fiction. The story is of a spirited young American woman, Isabel Archer, who "affronts her destiny" and finds it overwhelming. She inherits a large amount of money and subsequently becomes the victim of Machiavellian scheming by two American expatriates. The narrative is set mainly in Europe, especially in England and Italy. Generally regarded as the masterpiece of his early phase, The Portrait of a Lady is described as a psychological novel, exploring the minds of his characters, and almost a work of social science, exploring the differences between Europeans and Americans, the old and the new worlds.

The second period of James's career, which extends from the publication of The Portrait of a Lady through the end of the nineteenth century, features less popular novels including The Princess Casamassima, published serially in The Atlantic Monthly in 1885–1886, and The Bostonians, published serially in The Century Magazine during the same period. This period also featured James's celebrated Gothic novella, The Turn of the Screw.

The third period of James's career reached its most significant achievement in three novels published just around the start of the 20th century: The Wings of the Dove (1902), The Ambassadors (1903), and The Golden Bowl (1904). Critic F. O. Matthiessen called this "trilogy" James's major phase, and these novels have certainly received intense critical study. It was the second-written of the books, The Wings of the Dove (1902) that was the first published because it attracted no serialization. This novel tells the story of Milly Theale, an American heiress stricken with a serious disease, and her impact on the people around her. Some of these people befriend Milly with honourable motives, while others are more self-interested. James stated in his autobiographical books that Milly was based on Minny Temple, his beloved cousin who died at an early age of tuberculosis. He said that he attempted in the novel to wrap her memory in the "beauty and dignity of art".

Shorter narratives

James was particularly interested in what he called the "beautiful and blest nouvelle", or the longer form of short narrative. Still, he produced a number of very short stories in which he achieved notable compression of sometimes complex subjects. The following narratives are representative of James's achievement in the shorter forms of fiction.

- "A Tragedy of Error" (1864), short story

- "The Story of a Year" (1865), short story

- A Passionate Pilgrim (1871), novella

- Madame de Mauves (1874), novella

- Daisy Miller (1878), novella

- The Aspern Papers (1888), novella

- The Lesson of the Master (1888), novella

- The Pupil (1891), short story

- "The Figure in the Carpet" (1896), short story

- The Beast in the Jungle (1903), novella

- An International Episode (1878)

- Picture and Text

- Four Meetings (1885)

- A London Life, and Other Tales (1889)

- The Spoils of Poynton (1896)

- Embarrassments (1896)

- The Two Magics: The Turn of the Screw, Covering End (1898)

- A Little Tour of France (1900)

- The Sacred Fount (1901)

- Views and Reviews (1908)

- The Wings of the Dove, Volume I (1902)

- The Wings of the Dove, Volume II (1909)

- The Finer Grain (1910)

- The Outcry (1911)

- Lady Barbarina: The Siege of London, An International Episode and Other Tales (1922)

- The Birthplace (1922)

Plays

At several points in his career James wrote plays, beginning with one-act plays written for periodicals in 1869 and 1871 and a dramatisation of his popular novella Daisy Miller in 1882. From 1890 to 1892, having received a bequest that freed him from magazine publication, he made a strenuous effort to succeed on the London stage, writing a half-dozen plays of which only one, a dramatisation of his novel The American, was produced. This play was performed for several years by a touring repertory company and had a respectable run in London, but did not earn very much money for James. His other plays written at this time were not produced.

In 1893, however, he responded to a request from actor-manager George Alexander for a serious play for the opening of his renovated St. James's Theatre, and wrote a long drama, Guy Domville, which Alexander produced. There was a noisy uproar on the opening night, 5 January 1895, with hissing from the gallery when James took his bow after the final curtain, and the author was upset. The play received moderately good reviews and had a modest run of four weeks before being taken off to make way for Oscar Wilde's The Importance of Being Earnest, which Alexander thought would have better prospects for the coming season.

After the stresses and disappointment of these efforts James insisted that he would write no more for the theatre, but within weeks had agreed to write a curtain-raiser for Ellen Terry. This became the one-act "Summersoft", which he later rewrote into a short story, "Covering End", and then expanded into a full-length play, The High Bid, which had a brief run in London in 1907, when James made another concerted effort to write for the stage. He wrote three new plays, two of which were in production when the death of Edward VII on 6 May 1910 plunged London into mourning and theatres closed. Discouraged by failing health and the stresses of theatrical work, James did not renew his efforts in the theatre, but recycled his plays as successful novels. The Outcry was a best-seller in the United States when it was published in 1911. During the years 1890–1893 when he was most engaged with the theatre, James wrote a good deal of theatrical criticism and assisted Elizabeth Robins and others in translating and producing Henrik Ibsen for the first time in London.

Leon Edel argued in his psychoanalytic biography that James was traumatised by the opening night uproar that greeted Guy Domville, and that it plunged him into a prolonged depression. The successful later novels, in Edel's view, were the result of a kind of self-analysis, expressed in fiction, which partly freed him from his fears. Other biographers and scholars have not accepted this account, however; the more common view being that of F.O. Matthiessen, who wrote: "Instead of being crushed by the collapse of his hopes [for the theatre]... he felt a resurgence of new energy."

Non-fiction

Beyond his fiction, James was one of the more important literary critics in the history of the novel. In his classic essay The Art of Fiction (1884), he argued against rigid prescriptions on the novelist's choice of subject and method of treatment. He maintained that the widest possible freedom in content and approach would help ensure narrative fiction's continued vitality.

59

James wrote many valuable critical articles on other novelists; typical is his book-length study of Nathaniel Hawthorne, which has been the subject of critical debate. Richard Brodhead has suggested that the study was emblematic of James's struggle with Hawthorne's influence, and constituted an effort to place the elder writer "at a disadvantage." Gordon Fraser, meanwhile, has suggested that the study was part of a more commercial effort by James to introduce himself to British readers as Hawthorne's natural successor.

When James assembled the New York Edition of his fiction in his final years, he wrote a series of prefaces that subjected his own work to searching, occasionally harsh criticism.

At 22 James wrote The Noble School of Fiction for The Nation's first issue in 1865. He would write, in all, over 200 essays and book, art, and theatre reviews for the magazine.

For most of his life James harboured ambitions for success as a playwright. He converted his novel The American into a play that enjoyed modest returns in the early 1890s. In all he wrote about a dozen plays, most of which went unproduced. His costume drama Guy Domville failed disastrously on its opening night in 1895. James then largely abandoned his efforts to conquer the stage and returned to his fiction. In his Notebooks he maintained that his theatrical experiment benefited his novels and tales by helping him dramatise his characters' thoughts and emotions. James produced a small but valuable amount of theatrical criticism, including perceptive appreciations of Henrik Ibsen.

With his wide-ranging artistic interests, James occasionally wrote on the visual arts. Perhaps his most valuable contribution was his favourable assessment of fellow expatriate John Singer Sargent, a painter whose critical status has improved markedly in recent decades. James also wrote sometimes charming, sometimes brooding articles about various places he visited and lived in. His most famous books of travel writing include Italian Hours (an example of the charming approach) and The American Scene (most definitely on the brooding side).

James was one of the great letter-writers of any era. More than ten thousand of his personal letters are extant, and over three thousand have been published in a large number of collections. A complete edition of James's letters began publication in 2006, edited by Pierre Walker and Greg Zacharias. As of 2014, eight volumes have been published, covering the period from 1855 to 1880. James's correspondents included celebrated contemporaries like Robert Louis Stevenson, Edith Wharton and Joseph Conrad, along with many others in his wide circle of friends and acquaintances. The letters range from the "mere twaddle of graciousness" to serious discussions of artistic, social and personal issues.

Very late in life James began a series of autobiographical works: A Small Boy and Others, Notes of a Son and Brother, and the unfinished The Middle Years. These books portray the development of a classic observer who was passionately interested in artistic creation but was somewhat reticent about participating fully in the life around him.

Reception

Criticism, biographies and fictional treatments

James's work has remained steadily popular with the limited audience of educated readers to whom he spoke during his lifetime, and has remained firmly in the canon, but, after his death, some American critics, such as Van Wyck Brooks, expressed hostility towards James for his long expatriation and eventual naturalisation as a British subject. Other critics such as E. M. Forster complained about what they saw as James's squeamishness in the treatment of sex and other possibly controversial material, or dismissed his late style as difficult and obscure, relying heavily on extremely long sentences and excessively latinate language. Similarly Oscar Wilde criticised him for writing "fiction as if it were a painful duty". Vernon Parrington, composing a canon of American literature, condemned James for having cut himself off from America. Jorge Luis Borges wrote about him, "Despite the scruples and delicate complexities of James, his work suffers from a major defect: the absence of life." And Virginia Woolf, writing to Lytton Strachey, asked, "Please tell me what you find in Henry James. ... we have his works here, and

I read, and I can't find anything but faintly tinged rose water, urbane and sleek, but vulgar and pale as Walter Lamb. Is there really any sense in it?" The novelist W. Somerset Maugham wrote, "He did not know the English as an Englishman instinctively knows them and so his English characters never to my mind quite ring true," and argued "The great novelists, even in seclusion, have lived life passionately. Henry James was content to observe it from a window." Maugham nevertheless wrote, "The fact remains that those last novels of his, notwithstanding their unreality, make all other novels, except the very best, unreadable." Colm Tóibín observed that James "never really wrote about the English very well. His English characters don't work for me."

Despite these criticisms, James is now valued for his psychological and moral realism, his masterful creation of character, his low-key but playful humour, and his assured command of the language. In his 1983 book, The Novels of Henry James, Edward Wagenknecht offers an assessment that echoes Theodora Bosanquet's:

> "To be completely great," Henry James wrote in an early review, "a work of art must lift up the heart," and his own novels do this to an outstanding degree ... More than sixty years after his death, the great novelist who sometimes professed to have no opinions stands foursquare in the great Christian humanistic and democratic tradition. The men and women who, at the height of World War II, raided the secondhand shops for his out-of-print books knew what they were about. For no writer ever raised a braver banner to which all who love freedom might adhere.

William Dean Howells saw James as a representative of a new realist school of literary art which broke with the English romantic tradition epitomised by the works of Charles Dickens and William Makepeace Thackeray. Howells wrote that realism found "its chief exemplar in Mr. James... A novelist he is not, after the old fashion, or after any fashion but his own." F.R. Leavis championed Henry James as a novelist of "established pre-eminence" in The Great Tradition (1948), asserting that The Portrait of a Lady and The Bostonians were "the two most brilliant novels in the language." James is now prized as a master of point of view who moved literary fiction forward by insisting in showing, not telling, his stories to the reader. (Source: Wikipedia)

NOTABLE WORKS

NOVELS

Watch and Ward (1871)

Roderick Hudson (1875)

The American (1877)

The Europeans (1878)

Confidence (1879)

Washington Square (1880)

The Portrait of a Lady (1881)

The Bostonians (1886)

The Princess Casamassima (1886)

The Reverberator (1888)

The Tragic Muse (1890)

The Other House (1896)

The Spoils of Poynton (1897)

What Maisie Knew (1897)

The Awkward Age (1899)

The Sacred Fount (1901)

The Wings of the Dove (1902)

The Ambassadors (1903)

The Golden Bowl (1904)

The Whole Family (collaborative novel with eleven other authors, 1908)

The Outcry (1911)

The Ivory Tower (unfinished, published posthumously 1917)

The Sense of the Past (unfinished, published posthumously 1917)

SHORT STORIES AND NOVELLAS

A Tragedy of Error (1864)

The Story of a Year (1865)

A Landscape Painter (1866)

A Day of Days (1866)

My Friend Bingham (1867)

Poor Richard (1867)

The Story of a Masterpiece (1868)

A Most Extraordinary Case (1868)

A Problem (1868)

De Grey: A Romance (1868)

Osborne's Revenge (1868)

The Romance of Certain Old Clothes (1868)

A Light Man (1869)

Gabrielle de Bergerac (1869)

Travelling Companions (1870)

A Passionate Pilgrim (1871)

At Isella (1871)

Master Eustace (1871)

Guest's Confession (1872)

The Madonna of the Future (1873)

The Sweetheart of M. Briseux (1873)

The Last of the Valerii (1874)

Madame de Mauves (1874)

Adina (1874)

Professor Fargo (1874)

Eugene Pickering (1874)

Benvolio (1875)

Crawford's Consistency (1876)

The Ghostly Rental (1876)

Four Meetings (1877)

Rose-Agathe (1878, as Théodolinde)

Daisy Miller (1878)

Longstaff's Marriage (1878)

An International Episode (1878)

The Pension Beaurepas (1879)

A Diary of a Man of Fifty (1879)

A Bundle of Letters (1879)

The Point of View (1882)

The Siege of London (1883)

Impressions of a Cousin (1883)

Lady Barberina (1884)

Pandora (1884)

The Author of Beltraffio (1884)

Georgina's Reasons (1884)

A New England Winter (1884)

The Path of Duty (1884)

Mrs. Temperly (1887)

Louisa Pallant (1888)

The Aspern Papers (1888)

The Liar (1888)

The Modern Warning (1888, originally published as The Two Countries)

A London Life (1888)

The Patagonia (1888)

The Lesson of the Master (1888)

The Solution (1888)

The Pupil (1891)

Brooksmith (1891)

The Marriages (1891)

The Chaperon (1891)

Sir Edmund Orme (1891)

Nona Vincent (1892)

The Real Thing (1892)

The Private Life (1892)

Lord Beaupré (1892)

The Visits (1892)

Sir Dominick Ferrand (1892)

Greville Fane (1892)

Collaboration (1892)

Owen Wingrave (1892)

The Wheel of Time (1892)

The Middle Years (1893)

The Death of the Lion (1894)

The Coxon Fund (1894)

The Next Time (1895)

Glasses (1896)

The Altar of the Dead (1895)

The Figure in the Carpet (1896)

The Way It Came (1896, also published as The Friends of the Friends)

The Turn of the Screw (1898)

Covering End (1898)

In the Cage (1898)

John Delavoy (1898)

The Given Case (1898)

Europe (1899)

The Great Condition (1899)

The Real Right Thing (1899)

Paste (1899)

The Great Good Place (1900)

Maud-Evelyn (1900)

Miss Gunton of Poughkeepsie (1900)

The Tree of Knowledge (1900)

The Abasement of the Northmores (1900)

The Third Person (1900)

The Special Type (1900)

The Tone of Time (1900)

Broken Wings (1900)

The Two Faces (1900)

Mrs. Medwin (1901)

The Beldonald Holbein (1901)

The Story in It (1902)

Flickerbridge (1902)

The Birthplace (1903)

The Beast in the Jungle (1903)

The Papers (1903)

Fordham Castle (1904)

Julia Bride (1908)

The Jolly Corner (1908)

The Velvet Glove (1909)

Mora Montravers (1909)

Crapy Cornelia (1909)

The Bench of Desolation (1909)

A Round of Visits (1910)

OTHER

Transatlantic Sketches (1875)

French Poets and Novelists (1878)

Hawthorne (1879)

Portraits of Places (1883)

A Little Tour in France (1884)

Partial Portraits (1888)

Essays in London and Elsewhere (1893)

Picture and Text (1893)

Terminations (1893)

Theatricals (1894)

Theatricals: Second Series (1895)

Guy Domville (1895)

The Soft Side (1900)

William Wetmore Story and His Friends (1903)

The Better Sort (1903)

English Hours (1905)

The Question of our Speech; The Lesson of Balzac. Two Lectures (1905)

The American Scene (1907)

Views and Reviews (1908)

Italian Hours (1909)

A Small Boy and Others (1913)

Notes on Novelists (1914)

Notes of a Son and Brother (1914)

Within the Rim (1918)

Travelling Companions (1919)

Notebooks (various, published posthumously)

The Middle Years (unfinished, published posthumously 1917)

A Most Unholy Trade (1925, published posthumously)

The Art of the Novel : Critical Prefaces (1934)

CPSIA information can be obtained
at www.ICGtesting.com
Printed in the USA
LVHW091911191020
669186LV00003B/28

9 781662 719318